Biscuit's Sleepover

by ALYSSA SATIN CAPUCILLI

HarperFestival®
A Division of HarperCollins*Publishers*

Interior illustrations by Rosemary Berlin
Based on the illustration style of Pat Schories

Library of Congress catalog card number: 2007928023
13 14 15 16   LP/CWM   10 9 8 7 6
ISBN 978-0-06-112842-4
Typography by John Sazaklis
❖
First Edition

"Come along, Biscuit.
We're going to sleep at Puddles's house.
It's our first sleepover!"
Woof, woof!

"We have our blankets and our dolls."
Woof, woof!

"Funny puppy!
You have your bone, too."

"Hooray! It's time for some sleepover fun!"
Bow wow!
Woof, woof!

"We can play lots of games.
We can share snacks.
There's a special snack, just for you two!"
Bow wow!
Woof!

"It's fun to tell stories at a sleepover.
Here, Biscuit!
You can sit on my lap."
Woof, woof!

"Come along, everybody.
Let's set up our beds for the sleepover!"
Bow wow!
"No tugging on the pillows, Puddles."

Woof, woof!
"No tugging on the blankets, Biscuit."

Bow wow!
Woof, woof!

"Oh, no!
Silly puppies!
No jumping on the bed!"

"Come along, now.
It's time to curl up.
It's time for bed!"
Woof, woof!
"Good night, Biscuit."

Bow wow!
"Good night, Puddles."

Woof, woof, woof, woof!
"Wait, Biscuit.

Where are you going?"
Woof, woof!
"Don't you want to sleep at Puddles's house?"
Woof!

"Here, sweet puppy.
This is our first sleepover.
But we can make a wish on the stars
and say goodnight to the moon, just like at home."
Woof, woof!

"Look, Biscuit!
We can curl up with our blankets and dolls,
just like at home, too."
Woof, woof!

"We can even put a picture
of Mom and Dad right by our side, Biscuit.
I can hardly wait to tell them
all about our first sleepover fun!"
Woof, woof!

"Sleepy puppies; sweet dreams!"
Bow wow!
Woof!